D0863247

Bronwen Wallace

Common Magic

Many of these poems first appeared in *Anything is Possible, Descant, Fireweed, Full Moon, Canadian Forum* and *The New Canadian Poets, 1970-85.*

The author wishes to thank both the Canada Council and the Ontario Arts Council for their financial assistance.

ISBN 0 88750 570 8 (hardcover)
ISBN 0 88750 571 6 (softcover)

Cover art by Herzl Kashetsky. Typesetting and design by Michael Macklem

Printed in Canada

PUBLISHED IN CANADA BY OBERON PRESS

With love and thanks to Anna-Marie, Carolyn, Isabel and Mary for their support and help, these poems are for my parents, Marguerite and Ferdinand, and my son, Jeremy.

THE TOWN WHERE I GREW UP

In the town where I grew up,
most of the people had ancestors
who were UELs and they still
liked things tidy, kept their yards
fenced and their noses clean.
After that, the things that mattered
most were last names
and being Protestant.

North of the town, the road
disintegrated into potholes and the dust
that weathered the grey shacks
where the grimy laundry flapping
in the trees was the flag
of another country.

Up there
people shooed the chickens
off the table when the pastor came.

Things happened.

Crops withered overnight, ramshackle
barns hid two-headed cattle and young
girls bore their fathers' children.

5

What went on up there
was a story in a foreign language.

Pieces of it drifted into town,
like scraps of paper, catching
on the neat white fences
in the shaded streets.

Them and us.

I used to believe this.
Used to imagine an invisible
border, like the Maginot Line
we learned about in school,
between the teeming farms
that bordered our town
and the bare-boned fields beyond
where the shacks grew.

Now I think it's merely
a matter of emphasis,
like the *Globe & Mail*
and the *National Enquirer*.
They're both the same, really;
they both line words
like bars across the pages,
making you want to squeeze
between them into the white
where you think the truth is.

6

Each spring the countryside
fills up with lilacs. Every house
in town, every farm, every shack
has a clump of white or purple
at the doorstep. And on the road north,
bushes occur in the fields, alone,
not a house in sight for miles.
You might think they'd grown wild,
but you'd be wrong. Planted for good luck
by the early settlers, the lilacs continue
long after the farms fail and houses
weather away.

Flags of a different kind.

They indicate the subterranean counties
plotted underneath the sleekest pastures,
the sanest red-brick houses.
And rooted in the littered dark,
as dreams are, they bloom
each May as if they were
the only living things on earth.

LONELY FOR THE COUNTRY

Sometimes these days
you think you are ready
to settle down.

This might be the season for it,
this summer of purple sunsets
when you stand in the streets
watching the sky, until its colour
is a bruised place
inside your chest.

When you think of settling down
you imagine yourself growing comfortable
with the land and remember the sunstained faces
of men like your grandfather, the ridges of black veins
that furrowed the backs of their hands as they squared
a county boundary for you, or built once more
old Stu McKenzie's barn exactly as they'd raised it
60 years ago.
You watch the hands of the women
on market days, piling onions, filling buckets
with tomatoes, their thick, workaday gestures
disclosing at times
what you think you recognize as caring,
even love.

At least that's how it looks
from the outside and when you think
of settling down, you always think of it
as a place.

8

It makes the city seem imaginary, somehow.
As you drive through the streets,
you begin to see how the lives there look
as if they had been cut from magazines:
a blond couple carrying a wicker picnic-basket
through the park, a man in faded brown shorts
squatting on his front lawn
fixing a child's red bike.

You wish you could tell yourself
that this is all too sentimental.
You want to agree with the person
who said, "There's no salvation
in geography."

But you can't
and you're beginning to suspect
that deep within you,
like a latent gene, is this belief
that we belong somewhere.

What you know
is that once you admit that
it opens in you
a deeper need.
A need like that loneliness
which makes us return again and again
to the places we've shared
with those we can no longer love,
empty-hearted, yet expectant,
searching for revelations
in the blank faces of remembered houses.

As wide as bereavement
and dangerous,
it renders us innocent
as mourners at a graveside
who want to believe their loss
has made this holy ground
and wait
for the earth beneath their feet
to console them.

10

PLACE OF ORIGIN

One by one my friends move away
to become legends. What news I have of them
arrives like postcards with foreign stamps
or those messages that always look
as if the person who wrote them
was thinking of something else the whole time.

Me, I keep on living here, without meaning to.
Friends ask me why, I say *light*,
I say *lake*, I say *cost of housing*,
but it doesn't add up and most of them know it.
The ones who don't tell me how nice it must be
to feel rooted. Like an oak tree
or as if my feeling for the place
were something I could cultivate
as easily as turnips or potatoes.
Other people take me to the mountains,
or try to make me love an ocean,
but all I can see are more postcards.
"Too fancy for me," I tell them,
trying to keep it casual,
but my face muscles start to rearrange themselves:
my grandfather's look, half-sullen, half-sly
whenever anyone would mention Toronto or Montreal.
The look that told you most people were tourists to him
and there was nothing he could do about it.
(Meaning, he didn't want to.
Meaning, he'd never been twenty miles from his hometown
and that was enough for him.)

For most places, there are two kinds of geography
and it's no different here.
The men know land and weather,
who owns it and for how long,
what to prepare for when you can.
Being men, they have access to maps
and county records, almanacs.
Their wives know it differently.
Not just who married who
but what it was like and why,
how the kids turned out in the end.
This may be gossip,
but that doesn't make it unimportant.
You can't have your daughters marrying men
who beat their wives, raising children
who will tear all over the countryside
making fools of themselves.
"What's bred in the bone," my grandmother said,
"comes out in the flesh."

All of which I can accept, like the look
in my mother's eyes these days
when she tells me of another wedding or another death,
saying it's time for you to learn all this.
(Meaning, some day you have to decide
what you're doing here.)
But I'm not sure I want it.
I could tell you that this place
holds me like a family and mean it,
but that also means it holds me back.
These people who know who I am, who I've been,
       for generations
assume a certain ownership
and the hard part is, I recognize their right.

I wanted something simpler,
a place of origin,
direct as the love I imagined feeling for the dead,
believing grief made love perfect.
But even the dead go on changing,
whether I want to admit it or not,
there's always another coming to terms
and another.

My friends keep on asking
what I'm doing here and I keep on
not having the answer.
The thing I worry about most though
is that my children are getting older
and I could get stuck here
through another generation, without meaning to.
The thing I keep seeing is my grandfather's face,
letting you know that Toronto and Montreal
were nothing to him, he belonged right here.
Bluffing you
into believing it.

DISTANCE FROM HARROWSMITH TO TAMWORTH

Beside me, Jeremy is searching for the North West Territories,
white with red letters in the shape of a polar bear.
It's all he needs to complete Canada,
though he won't find it here on 38,
only a few tourists heading north to cottage country,
the rest, local traffic,
people who've no place else to go but home.

The farm where my father was born
is on the left, a mile outside of Harrowsmith,
my grandfather too, and my great-grandfather.
Now my cousin's there with his new wife
and already the old barns square their shoulders,
the silos straighten, eager for the birth of a son,
they seem to crowd the house, as if there's still not
    room enough
to separate love from geography.

Like the back of my hand, we say
for the place we come to call home,
the claim we can only make
through the hands, planting food and children.

14

Even my two gripping the steering-wheel
know this road as a hunger I can't help
giving in to: "'Look," I say to Jeremy
as we pull into Hartington, "there's the school
where your grandmother taught before she met Grandpa,"
baiting him, hoping he'll bite for the rest of the story,
though I'll tell it anyway. His grandmother, from Enterprise,
just happening to get that school, just happening
to board at the farm across the way,
which belonged to some uncle or other of his grandfather's
who was helping out there for a bit,
as if he were meant to meet her, I want to say, make him hear
the story the way I did—how he was slopping pigs
    that first day
when she came up the lane, so that she thought he was the
    hired man
and said that at dinner, everyone laughing at her—
how it seemed to me then that the distance between
Enterprise and Hartington was immense, impossible, amazing
to discover that out of all those back roads and
    misunderstandings
and incomprehensible adult laughter should come my mother
    and my father.

I'm still trying to explain it when we turn west at Verona,
but I've hardly finished a sentence before
we're at Bellrock, where my father's mother was born
and moved from, to another farm on 38, just in time
to meet my grandfather, and after Bellrock,
Enterprise, the very house my mother lived in as a girl,
twenty minutes from Hartington, at the most,
but, oh Jeremy, so much farther really.
Listen, I try to say, *listen!*
This is the most important story
you will ever hear.

Except that it isn't
and Jeremy leans forward, playing with the radio.
He has his own magic parent, after all;
his father lives 400 miles away,
arrives on a black Yamaha for technicolour weekends;
even the long times in between are filled
with the tapes they send instead of letters
once a week, Jeremy alone in his room
talking to a machine and able to make it sound
like an ordinary conversation.
Who am I to say what distances he should believe in,
these towns rush together, like my words or the fields
he swims through, so much green noise.

In the ditches *Purple Loosestrife, Horseweed,*
Fleabane, St. John's Wort, names I learned only this year
to make the flowers more familiar. Like these stories,
all I have to call a country,
rich as blood, placenta for my future
already seeded in the fields or that woman's face
in the last town, the curve of the road there
as it turns toward the next, *Tamworth* people say
for this one, needing something
to make it sound like a choice,
whatever holds them here,
whatever they've come to love enough.

16

MY SON IS LEARNING TO INVENT

My son is learning to invent
himself. Today he tells me of a time
I took him to a hospital and left him
alone there. He describes how he shook the steel
bars of his crib and cried as I left the room
without looking back.

(He was three. He had pneumonia
and I was alone. For a week,
I slept in a chair by his bed.
I only left once to buy him a book
when he was asleep.
The child in the next bed
had tubes in her throat and no-one
came to visit her at all.)

My son holds up his hands. If he could,
he would show me the desperate
welts the crib bars left and the black
square of my back cutting the light
from his eyes.

But I shake my head.

Stalemate.

17

Sometimes I show him pictures of myself
when I was his age. There is one
where I sit with my kid brother
in the middle of my grandfather's garden.
This is the one my son likes best.
But he insists that the boy,
my brother, who is fat and freckled,
is himself.

"Don't be ridiculous," I tell him,
"that's your Uncle Cam."

He tosses the photograph aside
and refuses to lose himself
in family history. What good is it
to him? Like that stupid riddle
about the sound of a tree falling
alone in a forest of trees.
The sun that shines over
these other children's heads
might as well be shining over
an empty pasture for all he cares.

In the top right corner of the photograph
is the cornfield where the children played
hide-and-go-seek.
We are still there, of course,
only now it is my son and I
who stalk each other
through the thin, green
leaves that bristle our bare arms
and whisper as they fold behind us, dry
secrets only they understand.

Whose childhood is this, anyway?

When we play in the park, he rides
in a swing so high above my head
the peak of his cap is a dark arrow
aimed at the heart of the sun.

"Look!" he calls.

And he lets go.

Only his body sinks through the abrupt
air toward concrete and the horrible
sound my throat can't make.

When the rest of the park
begins to move again
he is sprawled on his stomach
in the grass beyond the swing.

He gets to his feet
and his face is the colour of milk,
his lips sucked in
like an old man's.

I open my mouth, as he looks
up at me, wiping his palms on his jeans.
"Were you scared?" he asks.

My son is learning.

19

INTO THE MIDST OF IT

You'll take a map, of course, and keep it
open in front of you on the dashboard,
though it won't help. Oh, it'll give mileages,
boundary lines, names, that sort of thing,
but there are places yet
where names are powerless
and what you are entering
is like the silence words get lost in
after they've been spoken.

It's the same with the highways.
The terse, comforting numbers
and the signs that anyone can read.
They won't be any good to you now.
And it's not that kind of confidence
you're after anyway.

What you're looking for are the narrower,
unpaved roads that have become
the country they travel over, dreamlike
as the spare farms you catch
in the corner of your eye,
only to lose them
when you turn your head. The curves
that happen without warning
like a change of heart,
as if, after all these journeys,
the road were still feeling
its way through.

A man comes up on your right—blue shirt
patched from the sky—solid and
unsurprised. He doesn't turn his head
at your passing and by the time your eyes move
to the rear-view mirror, the road has changed.
But it's then you begin to notice
other people: women hanging clothes from grey
porches, a clutter of children on the steps.
Like the man, they do not move
as you go by and you try to imagine
how you must look to them: metallic glimmer
on the bright rim of their sky,
disturbing the dust
that settles behind you, slowly,
through the day's heat,
while in your mind's eye, their faces
form and change with the rippling patterns
sun and cloud make on the fields,
like the figures that swim below your thoughts
in the hour between dream and waking.

It makes you think of the people you love,
how their faces look when they don't know you're
    watching them,
so that what you see there
forces you to recognize
how useless your love is, how little
all your hopes, your good intentions
can ever do for them.

Only now, this doesn't hurt any more,
becomes part of your love, in a way,
just as the dry-weather drone of the cicada
belongs to the heat, to the dust that sifts
like ash over the shiny leaves,

this country you're travelling through,
where the farmlands draw their nourishment
from an ancient mountain range,
and houses rise, insistent
as the rock and almost as indifferent,
making all your questions
about why people came here,
what they liked about it,
why they stayed
as meaningless as questions you might ask
of the trees or the earth itself.

You, who have lived your whole life believing
if you made enough plans
you wouldn't need to be afraid,
driving through a countryside
only the road seems to care about,
to rediscover every time it enters
with that kind of love that's partly tenderness
and partly a sort of confidence
you can't put words around.
Like the look
the people at home will give you
when you get there: nonchalant and almost too deep
for you to see, as they turn back
to whatever held them
before you came.

MEXICAN SUNSETS

Somewhere in Mexico, a volcano erupts,
spewing dust that drifts northward
disturbing the atmosphere of Southern Ontario
so that all this autumn, small, grey
English-speaking towns are startled
by inordinate sunsets: shameless
fuchsias, brazen corals flaunt
their outlandish origins in a country
where anything can happen.

Nothing's the same any more.
Here in Kingston, even limestone forgets itself
and the staid Protestant church towers
succumb to gothic fantasies, windows ablaze
with dragons' fire and the pink screams
of captured damsels; while the bare, old
branches of trees are elegant filigrees,
burnt black and delicate
by so much colour.

It's November, but no-one believes it.
Winter's a crass rumour like the threat
of a layoff or a government's economic policy.
And the people inhabiting the lavender streets
have the stature of fabled creatures
from that land we all believe in, somewhere
between imagination and nostalgia.

You could call it
a state of grace, although
it's only for a season, like the love
we risk for each other
on the first fine day in March,
or during the perfect anarchy
of a heavy snowfall
when everyone's late for work
and doesn't give a damn.

A kind of conspiracy
we let ourselves get caught in,
half-bewildered, half-encouraged
by the sky's extravagance, this
fragile crust of earth
pulsing beneath us.

COMMON MAGIC

Your best friend falls in love
and her brain turns to water.
You can watch her lips move,
making the customary sounds,
but you can see they're merely
words, flimsy as bubbles rising
from some golden sea where she
swims sleek and exotic as a mermaid.

It's always like that.
You stop for lunch in a crowded
restaurant and the waitress floats
toward you. You can tell she doesn't care
whether you have the baked or french-fried
and you wonder if your voice comes
in bubbles too.

It's not just women either. Or love
for that matter. The old man
across from you on the bus holds
a young child on his knee; he is singing
to her and his voice is a small boy
turning somersaults in the green
country of his blood.
It's only when the driver calls his stop
that he emerges into this puzzle
of brick and tiny hedges. Only then
you notice his shaking hands, his need
of the child to guide him home.

All over the city
you move in your own seasons
through the seasons of others: old women, faces
clawed by weather you can't feel
clack dry tongues at passersby
while adolescents seethe
in their glassy atmospheres of anger.

In parks, the children
are alien life-forms, rooted
in the galaxies they've grown through
to get here. Their games weave
the interface and their laughter
tickles that part of your brain where smells
are hidden and the nuzzling textures of things.

It's a wonder that anything gets done
at all: a mechanic flails
at the muffler of your car
through whatever storm he's trapped inside
and the mailman stares at numbers
from the haze of a distant summer.

26

Yet somehow letters arrive and buses
remember their routes. Banks balance.
Mangoes ripen on the supermarket shelves.
Everyone manages. You gulp the thin air
of this planet as if it were the only
one you knew. Even the earth you're
standing on seems solid enough.
It's always the chance word, unthinking
gesture that unlocks the face before you.
Reveals the intricate countries
deep within the eyes. The hidden
lives, like sudden miracles,
that breathe there.

27

CHARLIE'S YARD

Some things have an order
that isn't planned. In Charlie's yard
the woodpile leans toward the necessary
laws of gravity enough to keep it
upright, but its true symmetry comes
more from anger: clean bite of it
and axe in Charlie's hands,
driving deep into the sullen heart
of a solitary night. After his wife left
the only things that Charlie brought
from the farm they'd shared
were bits of machinery, scraps he liked
the shapes and colours of. They rust in the green
of his garden, plough discs and waggon wheels.
Each one has its place somehow, an authority
tranquil as an old man's, who has worked
all his life with his hands, until even his mind
moves around thoughts with the same
unhurried grace. It's like that wicker chair
abandoned in the middle of the yard. No-one intended
to leave it there, just drifted off toward
whatever plans they'd made while sitting in it.

Now, it's rooted there as surely
as the tree behind it, weathered into place
like the bare grey boards of the tool-shed.
Some things have an order
that isn't planned. They seem aimless
as the hours a man spends waiting
for the woman he loves,
a pot of coffee going muddy on the stove.
It's just when he's given up
he turns to find her, framed by the white
wood of his doorway and the blue sky
caught in her hair.

COMING THROUGH

It's the time of day you like best: that hour
just before dark, when the colours
and shapes of things seem to forget
their daylit boundaries, so that the sound
of someone whistling in the street is the last pink
light on the horizon, fading through other sounds
of traffic and laughter into lilac, into blue-grey.

Nothing is solid now. Against the sky the trees
are so still they vibrate with the effort
of holding themselves in and the walls of the houses
hesitate as if they might dissolve,
revealing the lives behind them, intricate
and enchanted as the lives of dolls.

You had a friend who opened
secrets for you like that
and when you think of her now
it's mostly on evenings like this one,
when the last of that light
which is itself a kind of silence
gives to the room a mirror-like quality,
translucent as a memory.

You can almost smell the coffee you'd make for her then,
see the steam rising from the blue cup, her fingers
curled around it, warming themselves.
You can still see the way her hands moved
when she talked, creating a second language,
drawing you in
to the very centre of her words
where the real stories lived.

And her eyes, following your sentences
wherever they led,
until it seemed those nights
you entered each other's lives
as if they were countries,
not the superficial ones that maps create,
or ordinary conversation, but the kind
that twist and plummet underneath a day's events
like the labyrinths you followed as a child
or the new-made world that opened
for you alone when you discovered lying.

You lived within each other then
and each of those nights was a place
you inhabited together, a place
you thought you could return to always.

The headlights from a passing car outside
startle the bright ghosts that gather
in the corners of the room. It makes you remember
the bedroom you had as a child
and how you huddled under the covers like a snail,
watching the goblins who lived in the dresser drawers
glide across the mirror and over the ceiling
into your bed. It was the smell of your teddy bear
that saved you then and the satin edge of the blanket
at your cheek as smooth as sleep.
It was the voices of your parents in the kitchen,
far away as growing up and as safe. Even by day
your parents filled their lives with such a confidence,
you believed they had been born into adulthood
or arrived there, years ago, before
there were any history-books or maps, and made it
their very own sort of place. Not like you.

Stubbing your toes on the furniture that changed
overnight, your arms suddenly appearing
from the sleeves of your favourite jacket
like a scarecrow's,
like somebody else.
You can laugh at it now, although
it's only lately you've begun to realize
how much of your time you've spent like that:
almost a guest in your own life,
wandering around waiting for someone
or something to explain things to you.

It was always late when she left
and you'd stand in the doorway, waiting
till she'd started the car, then
sit in the dark yourself
for the twenty minutes or so it took her
to drive home. As you locked up, checked the kids
you could imagine her doing the same thing,
so that on those nights sleep was just another opening,
another entry you made together.

She's been dead for a long time now.
You'd thought that would make a difference,
but it hasn't. And though you feel angry
at your need for an explanation
it's still there. As if she owed it to you somehow.
As if somebody did.

32

Oh, you've learned the accepted wisdom of it.
Can even feel yourself healing these days, almost
strong enough now to re-enter the place
you inhabited together. And you know
you'll never figure it all out anyway;
any more than you can understand your neighbours
from what you see in their lighted windows
framed, like public advertisements.

And yet.

A part of you resists all that.
Resists it with the pure, unthinking stubbornness
you lived in as a child,
that harder wisdom
you are rediscovering now.
Some people are a country
and their deaths displace you.
Everything you shared with them
reminds you of it: part of you in exile
for the rest of your life.

33

DAILY NEWS

There are days when I try to imagine the planet
pausing once in a while, like an old woman
on the edge of her bed, who sounds her bones
for the reaches her dying has made
while she slept.

These are the times when I believe
that old men do remember keener weather,
that January when their words froze in the air
or an August so blank with heat
that all it left was the smell
of the crops drying in the fields.
"It's all out of kilter now," one of them tells me,
"just more of the same all year round,"
and I want to believe the planet feels this
as a falling away she wants to tell us about
before it's too late.

Last week, a 20,000-year-old mastodon tusk
was washed up on Virginia Beach.
I believe we should take this
as a direct warning, or better still
a cry for help.

What I want most to believe, though,
is that we're all in this together.

As it is, I hardly know what to look for.
The birthrate's rising slightly, but
according to a recent survey
most teenagers can't see the point
of planning for the future.
Even my friends don't seem to feel
that what they're living these days
is a real life.

Instead, I hear men telling me
that victory is a nuclear war
which 60 million people survive.
I think they really believe this
and what's more, I'm sure it's nothing
to what they can do
whenever they want.

This is the point where I realize
how arrogant it is
to imagine the planet caring about all this.
Though I admit to the image
of a bitter woman longing for a death
that takes her whole family with her,
the mastodon tusk should be enough
to let us know
we're only another species after all.

Meanwhile, my son says he gets scared sometimes
on the way home from school
that they'll drop the bomb
before he makes it.
The worst part though
is how his voice is
when he tells me this.
How he doesn't ask
what he can do about it.

Meanwhile, I read in the papers
that they found a skeleton
that proves whales used to live on land.
And on another page, how doctors managed
to replace a man's left hand with his right
after both were cut off in an accident.
It's going to be okay too, although
"it looks very strange," the man reports.
"Suddenly I'm looking at a hand with fingers.
A hand. It's like getting married
to someone you don't know."

36

REMINDER

In a crowded theatre lobby, the perfume
in a strange woman's hair nudges a jealousy
I thought I'd put down years ago.
Unlocks that stubborn convolution of my brain
where it rears and spits.
Even my fingers turn to claws.

Smells like fists.
One whiff of feta cheese and olives
numbs my solar plexus with the blow of a first love,
while fresias are a falling into something deeper,
a loss I haven't even named yet.

I'm told that smell is centred
in our first brain. Primitive,
lizard part of us still cautiously sniffing
its way through colours and mysteries.
The world as it is before we discover
how to shape it into names,
learn to use language like a hope
for the future. Something that could save us
if we use it carefully, put enough words
between ourselves and the past.

A man and a woman sit in an all-night
restaurant. She's smoking cigarettes,
he's drinking cup after cup
of black coffee, double sugar.
They're in one of those conversations
you don't need words to follow,
though they're using enough of them, their mouths
so rigid with choosing that the lips
have thinned to that whiteness you find
outside pain, if you tighten your muscles hard enough.

And maybe it's only because I can't hear
what they're saying that I imagine
this other sound, somewhere between a feeling
and a voice. An ache in the bone that sings
of an old wound. Something you can't put
your finger on. Right now, it's cautionary,
like a growl, though already their bodies
cringe at it and their hands ride
the waves of its swelling.

Sooner or later it will
rise and she'll start screaming;
he'll retreat into that baffled
silence men sometimes use for tears.

38

This isn't a lesson in body-language.
It's more like a warning, though there's not
much we can do. We can't go back
to nuzzling and grunting at each other,
trying to sniff out anger or love.
And there's no such thing
as a simpler time anyway.

You might call it
a reminder, like the dinosaur
bone in the museum,
the one we can touch,
the one worn smooth
with our need.

Meanwhile, the man and woman go on
talking and I can imagine how their mouths
must ache for a word that's as explicit
as the click of her lighter,
his definitive way of measuring
the two teaspoonsful of sugar.
Words are their hope for the future.
They've cherished them like children.
And now their faces have the puzzled,
fragile look of parents
who have taken great care
and are always surprised
to see the past they thought
they'd freed their children from
assert itself. In their way of walking,
in their laughter,
in their sullen, indifferent eyes.

WOMAN AT THE NEXT

The woman at the next table is angry.
Angry in that dogged, repetitive way
a woman gets when she's had a few drinks.
Not enough to make her inarticulate,
but enough so that her voice has become something
you can feel, like the beginning of a headache,
at your temples or the back of your neck.

She's talking about men
and you've heard it all before:
in restaurants and elevators, at parties,
on a flight to Vancouver once, for five hours
the woman behind you going on and on.
Even the people she's with have stopped
trying to answer and are working hard
at being quiet and small.
Like children enduring a scolding
they look as if her voice has shoved them
into their seats and is holding them there.
Which it is, of course,
so that as you watch them, words and hands
get muddled in your mind
until they seem like the same thing.

40

Sometimes a person's hands
are the only words he knows.
A fat man sitting in a hospital waiting-room
after they have taken his wife
or his child away from him
bows his head beneath the doctor's level voice
and sees how the high, white vowels
of his clenched fists
begin in the darker sound
his heart is making.

Sometimes a man's words
are the holes he makes with these fists
in the brittle whine of his wife's complaint.
Everyone knows what a woman's scorn
is supposed to be like,
how we can eat a man with laughter
over a cup of coffee.

Which doesn't say much
for the woman at the next table.
Drunker now, her voice has gone teary and pale.
The only thing she'll want to eat tomorrow
are her own words.

41

That's what the people around her
are counting on: tomorrow
when she'll be right back
where she started, waiting on tables somewhere
or cleaning someone's house,
getting home late and ironing the kids' clothes
while she watches TV.
You can tell by her hands
that she works hard,
words are what she really binges on,
like someone cheating on a diet,
putting some more fat
between herself and her pain.

What gets you, of course,
is that you recognize the tendency
though you hate to admit it.
Hate to think of all the nights
you've spent like that,
all the mornings
waking from this dream
of your own voice
to the fumbling memory,
dead weight on the day.

"Getting it off your chest," it's called
though you can see now
that it doesn't make any sense
pretending anger is something you catch
like a bad cold
and then throw off again
in a couple of weeks.

You used to believe there was too much
anger in the world.
Now you think maybe there isn't enough.
Not the kind you can use anyway.
The kind that strips things down
to the cleaned, bare bones, naked and efficient,
shaped to fit the hand like a weapon.

Maybe it's like that somewhere else,
but you suspect
a lot of nights are just like this one;
anger slurred to tears
tomorrow's hangover already coating the tongue.
The kind of night that sends you into the streets
half-hoping for an accident or a fire,
the sound of sirens slicing into it
stopping everything cold.

43

HOW IT WILL HAPPEN

In this town
it's times like these
make a woman realize exactly
how her job is going to destroy her.

It won't be an accident either.
The sudden sheering of metal or rock
that gets you in a factory, a mine.
Even now, the woman can feel it coming on
like one of those slow diseases
of the joint or the bone
that doctors diagnose in terms you recognize
as bigger words for dying.

Her job is to sit at a desk all day,
talking to people who come at her
through a smudged glass door
that gets kicked in every week or so
by someone who didn't get what they wanted
or someone else who realized suddenly
that they never would.

After eight hours
she can go home.
Which is the problem.
Which is what makes her think
that maybe they're right,
the people who say a woman gets too personal
in a job like this, a problem of hormones maybe,
something in the size of the breasts,
the position of the uterus.

She envies the younger girls.
The way they snap their desk drawers shut
at 4.30 sharp, snap open their makeup cases,
paint their lips bright red.

Their laughter comes
from a great distance,
the way she imagines it must sound
to the woman she saw at 3.45.
The woman whose husband hit her so hard
he broke her middle ear,
sending the sounds of her own screams back
in a roar of blood.

Women and children.
In a town like this
where there aren't enough factories
to keep them busy, the women
take welfare. Their kids
take to the streets, surviving
on small stuff
until something comes along
that's big enough
to put them in jail for a few years.
The woman sees eight or ten a day.
Boys mostly. About her son's age.
Usually they stare at the floor
while she talks to them, arms folded
over their chests. And even when they do
look her in the eye
all she can see any more
are the faces they've learned to wear
for high-school principals, truant officers,
youth workers, cops.

Reminds her of that game she used to play
at the cottage, in August, when there was nothing
left to do: hauling waterlogged wood
out of the bay, to push it
over the edge of the dock,
watch it sink again
into the thick, dull water.

Since this is a prison town
most of the guys you read about
on the front pages
are here somewhere.
So are their wives and kids,
like camp-followers,
waiting for the next move.
Lots of times though
the next move takes so long
that by the time the guy gets out
even on a day-pass,
the families have disappeared.
These are the ones the woman feels most sorry for;
so she takes them out to a show
or invites them home for dinner.

At Christmas it was Tyler.
His first day out in ten years.
The woman remembers two things:
the hours he spent just sitting in her kitchen
studying the pattern pale sun made
with the plants in the window and the smoke
from his cigarettes;
and the way he stared
at her daughter's breasts
when she poured him coffee.

46

At night when she lies down
a voice drones in her head, like one of those tapes
you can play by your pillow
to help you learn things while you sleep.

It's only a job, the voice tells her,
*only a job. And there's only
so much you can do
for people like that.
They have to learn
to help themselves.*
But each day still
heaves itself in, white and graceless.
The same faces set themselves against her
and her words stumble in a need
that has nothing to do with help at all.

In a town like this,
it's times like these
make a woman see more clearly
how it will happen.
It isn't a matter of keeping on
or quitting. Nothing as clear as that.
But the look
on her son's face when he says
he wants to be a cop or a prison guard
(though he's only fourteen and you can't tell
with boys his age) because he's sick
of all this wishy-washy bleeding
heart crap. Wants to be a cop
so he can have things cut and dried.

It's watching him say that,
knowing he means it.
Knowing she wants the same thing herself.
Only differently.

DREAMS OF RESCUE

In the dream
the car is a sound,
a screech of brakes that tears a hole
in the sunlight, big enough
for the dog to flop through, fish-like
guts spilling on the side of the road.

In the dream
the children's voices
crying *do something do something*
are a mist I grope through, fingers thick
as my tongue with the smell of dust and blood.

A telephone grows from my hand
and my cry for help recedes into the churn
and whining of machinery
that rings
and rings
and rings
me into 3-AM darkness, cold
floor under my feet
and your voice
coming at me from the coast.

"Pour yourself a drink," you say,
"I'm paying."

It's only midnight where you are
two hours into a bottle and your second
pack of cigarettes, but there's no use arguing
and somehow the scotchI pour
cuts through time-zones and Prairie winters
until night and distance
are another room in this house
we are learning to build: two women
sitting up late, sharing out our days
with the whisky and the cigarettes.

Something has happened to you.
In your voice it's a kind of tenderness
that hovers over your words—like a mother
watching her kid learn to walk—
as if you could protect them
from what they must say.

You're telling me what you're reading
these days, titles I recognize, names.
Each one flares for a moment, struck match
that pulls some reassuring object
—watch-face, ashtray, scotch bottle—
out of the darkness
where your face bobs, white and scared.

Little sister.
When you were three
you were a pain in the ass.
All that summer at the cottage
watching you, waiting for you
and then that one morning for one moment
turning my back and turning again
to find you face down in the water.

I wouldn't call it love that pulled you
up by the arm and thumped you on the back
so hard your head snapped,
shook you till your face streamed snot
and tears, till you screamed, till you promised
never to tell, till I couldn't see you for the sun
and the sound of my own crying, fist
in the guts that taught me for the first time
how words like that are just a clumsy warning
scrawled at the border of a terrifying country.

Little sister:
most of the time you were just that.
A royal pain in the ass.
When I left for college
you were still playing dress-up;
it's only lately we've become
like any women,
starting from scraps of the past
and the rest of our lives
trying to find words that fit.

This pause that stretches between us now
is a tightrope, taut wire alive with waiting,
click of your lighter
catch in your breath
as you exhale smoke
begin:

" We're splitting, Carl and I."

50

"A lot of things. He   he tried
to beat me up, hit me with his fists
at first, we got a marriage counsellor
but

    (First, he hit you with his fists.
    First, he hit you.)

"but then he   he came at me
with a hammer   tore my shoulder
broke my nose . . .

"I've been in one of those houses
you know   for battered women . . .

"Pretty good   met some women here
it's all right   I'm okay
now   I . . .

Your voice falls away from me
into the lie you couldn't possibly finish
and like the cramped limb that wakes
the sleeper from a nightmare, stab of pain
in my palm, white grip of it
on the telephone receiver, pulls me up
into this room and if you were here, I swear
I could shake you till your head snapped.
Shake you the way a mother will shake a child
who has run beyond her into a scream
of brakes, as if she could shake her
into safety and herself free
of her own fierce helplessness.

51

You are crying now
and the sound reaches for me
through the distances
your husband's hands have forced
between us;
between what we must live
and what we can tell.

I think of all those proverbs
only a woman would use.
Our grandmother's cold comfort:

Marry in haste, repent at leisure.

You've made your bed. Now you must
lie in it.

Wisdom of women
whose only choice
was to choose someone else
and a lifetime at the halted limit
of that reaching.
All those dreams of rescue
we dreamed we'd put aside.

Your voice against all that.

Three thousand miles away
in a city I barely know
the man you love
has beaten you with a hammer
and if what needed to be said
were something a woman could make
from whatever she had on hand,

like a cut-down dress
like a good warm coat,
I would stay up all night
to finish it for you.

In the house that sheltered you
a woman's hands have rubbed your shoulders,
brought you tea and the names of lawyers,
the titles of books that might help.
And when you couldn't stand it,
when terror was a muffled weight
on your chest, thick as fur
over your mouth,
there was always a woman there
to hold you.

It means you'll survive all this
though we both know you'll never
get over it. There'll always be a need
for something tougher: a skin you could wrap
your heart in, fold it away
from this grieving that stuns you
with its news of a death.

"I only needed to hear your voice," you tell me.
"Just for a while. It's better now. Goodnight."

"Goodnight. Take care of yourself."

But sleep comes piecemeal,
teased by the goblin shapes
of what I could have, should have said.

I will be glad for morning,
for the brief light that delivers us
into its own kind of certainty
where the dream you woke me from
becomes a message I can puzzle over.
While the love I feel for you now
is like the story a mother tells her child
at bedtime, knowing it only serves
to carry her into a land of strangers
where she must dream her own rescue
from whatever scraps and fragments of it
she finds, wrecked there.

54

TO GET TO YOU

It's never easy.
Even the effort of a few steps
from the bedroom to the kitchen, say,
or a few muscles, opening my eyes
to find you still there in bed beside me
is an act of magic or faith,
I'm never sure which.

All I know is that it's learned
by doing, over and over again,
like any other trick,
until you don't need to think about it.
Like now. Like the way I'm walking home
to you through this city I've learned to accept
as the only kind there is: five o'clock,
night coming down and rain
just hard enough
to make the crowds on the corners shove a little
when a bus finally splashes to the stop.
Outside a restaurant, two men shake hands
and a little boy holds his father's
as they watch a toy airplane turning in a shop window.
It could be anywhere. But what I want you to notice
are the women. They are wearing white nurses' shoes,
or dirty sneakers or high-heeled boots.
They carry briefcases and flowers, bags of groceries
as they hurry home to their husbands and kids,
lovers, ailing parents, friends.
We all have the same look somehow.

See: over there by the bank
how that stout woman lowers her eyes
when she passes that group of boys,
how her movement's mimed
by the blonde, turning her head
when a car slows down beside her.
Even the high-pitched giggle of the girls
in that bunch of teenagers is a signal
I've learned to recognize. Tuned in
on my own tightened muscles, jawline or shoulders.
In fact, you might study the shoulders.
The line of the backbone too; arms and hips,
the body carried
like something the woman's not sure what to do with.

I've already told you that this is an ordinary city.
There are maps of it and lights to show us
when to walk, where to turn.
What I want you to know is that it isn't enough.

On a trip to Vancouver once
I discovered clearer landmarks. Red ones,
sprayed on sidewalks all over the city.
They marked the places
where a woman had been raped,
so that when I stepped out of a coffee shop
to find one on the pavement by the laundromat
geography shifted.
Brought me to the city I'd always imagined
happening in dark alleys, deserted parking-lots,
to somebody else. Brought me home in a way,
no longer the victim of rumours or old news,
that red mark planted in the pavement
like the flag of an ancient, immediate war.

I used to hope it was enough
that you are gentle,
that I love you,
but what can enough mean any more,
what can it measure?

How many rapes were enough
for those women in Vancouver
before they got stencils and spray paint
made a word for their rage?
How many more until even that word
lost its meaning
and the enemy was anything that moved out there.
Anything male, that is.

How can any woman say
she loves a man enough
when every city on the planet
is a minefield
she must pick her way through
just to reach him?

It's not that we manage it though.
It's that we make it look so easy.
These women wearing their fear
like a habit of speech or movement
as if this were the way
the female's body's meant to be.
The way I turn the last corner now,
open the door to find you
drinking wine and reading the newspaper,
another glass already filled
and waiting on the coffee-table.

When I turn on the hall light
the city will retreat into the rain,
the tiny squares of yellow
marking the other rooms
where men and women greet each other.
It's a matter of a few steps,
magic or faith, though it's not that simple.
The way the rain keeps watering the cities of the world.
How it throws itself against our window,
harder, more insistent,
so that we both hear.

58

THINKING WITH THE HEART

For Mary di Michele

"I work from awkwardness. By that I mean I don't like to arrange things. If I stand in front of something, instead of arranging it, I arrange myself"—Diane Arbus.

"The problem with you women is, you think with your hearts"—Policeman.

How else to say it
except that the body is a limit
I must learn to love,
that thought is no different from flesh
or the blue pulse that rivers my hands.
How else, except to permit myself
this heart and its seasons,
like the cycles of the moon
which never seem to get me anywhere
but back again, not out.

Thought should be linear.
That's what the policeman means
when I bring the woman to him,
what he has to offer for her bruises, the cut
over her eye: *charge him or we can't help you.*
He's seen it all before anyway. He knows
how the law changes, depending on what you think.
It used to be a man could beat his wife
if he had to; now, sometimes he can't

but she has to charge him
and nine times out of ten
these women who come in here
ready to get the bastard
will be back in a week or so
wanting to drop the whole thing
because they're back together,
which just means a lot of paperwork
and running around for nothing.
It drives him crazy, how a woman
can't make up her mind and stick to it,
get the guy out once and for all.
"Charge him," he says, "or we won't help."

Out of her bed then, her house, her life,
but not her head, no, nor her children,
out from under her skin.
Not out of her heart, which goes on
in its slow, dark way, wanting
whatever it is hearts want
when they think like this;
a change in his, probably,
a way to hold what the heart can't
without breaking: how the man who beats her
is also the man she loves.

I wish I could show you
what a man's anger makes
of a woman's face,
or measure the days it takes
for her to emerge from a map of bruises
the colour of death. I wish there were words
that went deeper than *pain* or *terror*
for the place that woman's eyes can take you
when all you can hear
is the sound the heart makes
with what it knows of itself
and its web of blood.

But right now, the policeman's waiting
for the woman to decide.
That's how he thinks of it; *choice*
or how you can always get what you want
if you want it badly enough.
Everything else he ignores,
like the grip of his own heart's red
persistent warning that he too is fragile.
He thinks he thinks with his brain
as if it were safe up there
in its helmet of bone
away from all that messy business
of his stomach or his lungs.
And when he thinks like that
he loses himself forever.

But perhaps you think I'm being hard on him,
he's only doing his job after all,
only trying to help.
Or perhaps I'm making too much of the heart,
pear-shaped and muscular, a pump really,
when what you want is an explanation or a reason.

But how else can I say it?
Whatever it is you need
is what you must let go of now
to enter your own body
just as you'd enter the room where the woman sat
after it was all over,
hugging her knees to her chest,
holding herself as she'd hold her husband
or their children, *for dear life*,
feeling the arm's limit, bone and muscle,
like the heart's.
Whatever you hear then
crying through your own four rooms,
what you must name for yourself
before you can love anything at all.

62

LIKE THIS

It's one of those moments we all recognize
sooner or later and always
in the midst of something
so mundane we aren't prepared
to have it open underneath our feet,
become the classic pratfall victims,
Coyote so intent on catching
Roadrunner he doesn't notice
he's walking on air past the edge
of the cliff. Right now we can watch
this man: slim, blond, mid-thirties,
sitting alone at the table, drinking a beer,
reading cookbooks. He's planning a dinner party
—the first one since his separation—
and he wants to use that recipe for
cucumber soup his wife used to make.
It'll be perfect for the meal
he's planned: glazed chicken and rice pilaf.

He can't find it, of course.
It's probably in one of the books she took
or scribbled on a piece of paper, stuck
in the back of a drawer in their old house.

He can also see there's lots of others
worth trying in these books.

He even knows he could call her up
and ask her for the goddamn recipe
if he wanted to.

Which he does.

But won't.

She'd give it to him.
He knows that.
And she wouldn't ask any questions either,
or make any tacky comments.
In fact, she'd probably be really pleased
to think he'd remembered.

And that's just it.
He tries to imagine the conversation, but
the words he'd have to use
and what they might mean
knot in his head
like the fist he feels
in his chest sometimes
when he thinks of her.

When the man hurls his beer bottle
at the kitchen wall,
the explosion of beer and glass
is almost as surprising
as the cry
that splits his throat
at the same time.

We half-expected it, of course,
just as we know that now,
a second later, the wet spot on the wall
begins to look foolish and the puddles
of beer and glass are just another mess
he'll have to clear
before his friends come.

We can see that
even as we understand
how good it felt.

As for the cry
and where it comes from,
we think we recognize that too,
but it won't help. Sooner or later
it'll be our turn. Face up against
the event in our own lives
that can't be expiated
and we'll forget about this man,
this voice we think we hear so
clearly now, saying,
Sorry,
saying, *Look, I've changed.*
Saying, *Isn't that enough?*

Well?

Isn't it?

65

SPLITTING IT UP

There's only so much anyone can say,
and after that it's almost a relief
to face the quieter expectations
our possessions have of us:
who'll take the wedding lamps, the antique rocker?
The kids' toys, divided in two piles,
one for each household.

In the kitchen, the bottom drawer's stuffed full
of paper bags and bits of tinfoil, waxed paper,
elastic bands. A habit learned from my mother's hands,
smoothing every scrap of a life
where nothing could be wasted.
All forgotten now, like the leftover food
going mouldy in the fridge.
We never could get the hang of it,
children of a richer age, how we hated
our parents' pale obsessions, the weight of things,
their cost, their quality,
their endless, inexplicable uses.

We divide the books and I carry another load
to the porch. Notice how the hinge still sticks
on the front door. I kick it open, awkward thing,
something you could have fixed if you'd wanted to.

66

It's only now—watching the familiar
duck of your head over a pile of papers,
sorting, choosing—only now I can begin to see
there's only so much anyone can do.
How so much of what we bring to a marriage
has its beginnings far outside our power
to alter or repair, though we bear the burden of it.
Like the hurt we carry away with us,
this furniture we share so scrupulously now,
knowing—though we do not say it—
that it will squat in corners the rest of our lives,
telling its own tales, singing its own histories.

67

RECLAIMING THE CITY

The sign says, *Windsor, City of Roses,*
but anyone who's lived here knows it's a city of hands
and dark metal, necessary as blood,
or the long lines of cars pumped from its factories
for the arteries of a continent.
A city of days produced on an assembly-line,
the sun an ancient star that doesn't chart things any more,
intruding on the dreams of those who churn with the effort
of learning this tighter chronology.
A city I came to by chance
the way I might meet a man at a party
and talk about anything at all,
never thinking he could change my life forever.
Which is not what I mean to say at all, of course;
a man at a party, putting this stranger in
as a mere figure of comparison
when what I need to say is, *you, you have,*
and what I want from this city now
is a sign, proof that I was a difference.

Tonight, I have dinner with Mark,
still in his apartment by the river.
More than anything, I envy his ease with the place,
love I want to call it, though he doesn't,
shrugging it off with that gesture
I've seen old men use for their wives,
as if what kept them in a marriage all their adult lives
were some paralysis they hadn't found a cure for yet.

He moved here in '67, just before the riots started in Detroit,
his balcony a ringside seat that summer
from which to watch the low hills of smoke
peaked occasionally by sirens or gunfire.
He kept his TV on the railing, tuning in particulars,
the recognizable curve of an arm throwing a bottle,
faces as young as his own, and the others, shielded by rifles
as the army moved in, but he turned the volume off,
he didn't want some newsman to explain things to him,
and now his stories stretch through pauses
more important than the words somehow,
like the fact that he's still sitting here,
taking it all in.

What we study tonight
is how Detroit has rebuilt itself, its skyline
dominated by RenCen, that space-age castle,
a city within a city, where tracks of light are elevators
carrying their passengers high into the night,
though in the older dark below
the planet is reclaiming its own,
block after block, as people move out to the suburbs
the grass moves back, bushes crowd from factories
and trees grow through the rooms of burnt-out houses.
In a few years, Mark says,
RenCen could be stranded in the middle of a forest,
an alien craft, with no-one to remember how it got there,
and tonight even the freighters on the river
move with more than their usual weariness
as if they've known all along
that their cargoes of oil or metal
are the lives of men and women, scrabbled from the earth
one way or another.

In this city where night is always
forcing someone out of bed and into a factory,
dreams come as they will
and if I could travel far enough
I'd find our place on Wyandotte,
just as it was, and you
leaving for work at midnight
while the baby and I curled into sleep,
milky with it, still, in the morning
when you returned, your anger cold as the first light.
All those nights punched in, punched out
to a language I couldn't love you enough to learn.
Any more than you could.
Tuned to your talk of unions and shop-floor politics,
how could you see that I was turning
to another revolution, how our son
tore my days up by their roots
and handed me a life I had to grow to fit
if I wanted to survive.

Statistically, it's common enough. *Marital breakdown
due to stress.* Science leaves us no-one
to blame any more; though in that, how is it different
from politics or religion, our own smaller wisdoms,
whatever brings me back here, hating
what this city made of us and keeps on making
of so many others. *City of Roses,*
though what thrives here is restlessness;
where someone is always working, anything can happen.

And a night like this drives a hard bargain;
it won't let me get away with feeling sorry,
that makeshift emotion I rig up sometimes
to disguise my choices. I'm stuck with what
I can't reclaim: how I loved you
as much as I love my life without you now
or my own body, our marriage in this city
we came to by chance, rooting ourselves
in the child we made, wanting to, not thinking of the future
as he carries us into it.

71

BLACKFLIES

For Jan Conn

You'd never use that word, of course,
but the one you have is as long as I am
and I can't remember it and anyway
what I really want to tell you is how much
you help me to remember
that language is never neutral.
I like to think it's because
you're both a poet and a scientist,
though all I have to go on, really,
is that peculiar undercurrent
in the rhythm of your speech, a caution
that comes from knowing words and scientific theories
are the tricks we have
for making the world fit
our view of it.

You spend the summer in Guatemala
collecting blackfly larvae and now
you describe your work using the language
of entomology, but they're still
just bugs to me, Jan, the kind that spoil
a weekend at the cottage in early June,
while *vector* and *nematode* place you
in my Grade-13 biology version of a laboratory
where you wear white and dissect things
and this gets all mixed up with
how a friend from Africa told me once
that when she first moved to Ontario it was the bugs
that nearly drove her mad and how surprised I was
because after all she was from *Africa*

where there are snakes that eat people, but
she just laughed and said she didn't
think of it like that.

You don't either.
Onchocerciasis is your word
for river blindness. It makes my skin twitch,
imagining parasites burrowing beneath it,
crawling up my spinal column to my brain
and the backs of my eyes.
A parasite carried by certain blackfly species,
which is the whole point, of course,
though I'm having trouble following you,
want you back in that crisp white lab
with lots of light, but your voice pulls me
out into some river in Guatemala, jungles and heat,
you standing there catching bugs and knowing
It's all useless, you say suddenly.
The government won't give a shit.
It's mainly the Indians who get it, after all.
And now, somewhere beyond you,
people are being shot and in the city
a man works all day for the dollar
that buys some rice or a half-pound of beans
for the children his wife carries
year after year, hoping
that one or two will survive.
It is hard to believe that so small a country
can contain so much horror,
though we never use that word
and *terrorism* is reserved for the bomb
that explodes without warning in a European city.

73

When you showed me the pictures you'd taken,
I almost laughed. A biologist's view of the place:
closeups of flower-buds and bugs on the undersides of leaves,
a country even smaller than the one my map shows
and more beautiful than it seems it ought to be.
Nothing fits. You spend years finding a cure
for river blindness and in a few quick generations
the parasites will adapt. It's the benefit
of having fewer chromosomes, you've told me,
evolution keeps us all on our toes, a black joke
like the way Chris is always saying
that when we finally kill ourselves off
the insects won't even notice.

For now though, they make me squeamish,
womanish, some might say, a description of my sex
that gets used as a term of derision.
And Jan, don't think this poem is all for you.
It grows out of my own need, this picture
I must invent of you in blue jeans
and a netted hat like the one my aunt wears
when she goes berry-picking.
You in the sweat and heat
moving through the water in that cautious way you have,
keeping your eyes and your hands focused,
your mind on the job.

74

But even the picture I invent
cannot make you larger,
a stroke as thin as a pencil
or a word against the grey
which I imagine as the colour of that country's sky;
though I know you've told me it is brilliant blue,
in *my* picture, Jan, in *my* picture it's dead
as the eyes of those who follow orders
no matter what they mean, a grey
that drains the colour from the land
until it seems you must raise your hands into fists.
But because this poem is for you, Jan,
that is not what will happen. Instead, I will invent you
bending beneath that sky, into the water
because that is what your job demands,
focusing on what your hand does best
because, like all of us, you must.

WHAT IT COMES TO MEAN

That we take so long to trust
even the most necessary facts,
our lack of power, for one thing,
or the body's patience in teaching us to die.
That we keep on thinking there's a limit
that will make things simple for us,
a once-and-for-all. *I'm done with that,*
my friend says of her divorce, *I've worked it out.*
She believes she can live in the present like that.
We all do.

The summer before Pat died
there was a night at my place
when a bat got in on us. It wouldn't stop
swooping round and round the room.
I had to kill it.
And afterwards, I wanted to stop
every crack in the building, got tape
and a step-ladder, half-crazy, trying to patch out chaos,
Pat on the couch refusing to help,
already knowing that it wouldn't.

I keep looking for a way round this,
an escape, a *worst,*
but even my dreams are houses
only birds find fit to live in,
walls shift and the roof sinks
through dust and wings.

76

The cries falling back to earth
are thin as the day they bring, another one
that won't protect me any more
from what I don't want to believe:
how every reckoning's a private, ragged thing
that rises, in the seasons of its need,
like Pat's breathing, on her last night,
tearing from the air the only silence
that would fit her, perfect
as her face, which I will never see again.

Sorrow wears itself a hollow,
cleans me out with its crying, a bare voice
like that weather our bones warn us about.
At first I thought it was malevolent,
something that *wouldn't* leave,
but now I know it is no different
from the light that washes in
and brings me my body back, an opening
that finds the people I love, still here,
yawning as they shrug the day on, matter-of-fact
as always, all of us a little puzzled
by our need for each other;
or the way Carolyn takes my hand in the middle of a walk,
laughing, as if it were nothing,
this gentleness we learn
from what we can't heal.

If I had a god,
I'd say we were holy and didn't know it,
but I see only what we make of ourselves on earth,
how long it takes for us to love what we are,
what we offer to each other only in our best moments,
but carelessly, without shyness,
like food grown in plenty,
our mouths blessed with it every day.

78

MELONS AT THE SPEED OF LIGHT

For Carolyn Smart

"Child," said the lion, "I am telling you your story, not hers.
No-one is told any story but their own"— *C.S. Lewis,*
A Horse and his Boy.

I keep having this dream
where the women I love swell up like melons,
    night after night.
It's not surprising, really.
They've reached that age
where a woman must decide once and for all,
and this summer most of them are pregnant.
Already their eyes have changed.
Like those pools you discover once in a while,
so deep with themselves
you can't imagine anything else swimming in them.
The eyes of pregnant women. The women I love
fallen into themselves, somehow, far beyond calling,
as if whatever swims in their bellies
were pulling them deeper and deeper.

I think that women's lives
are like our bodies.
Always at the mercy, you might say.
A woman turns 32 and her body lets her know
it's time to decide.
Or maybe she just loses her job and can't find another,
so she figures she might as well have the babies now as later.
The days become all mouth then
and everything smells of milk.

Her body goes a little vague at the edges
like it felt that time at summer camp
when she was learning how to hang in the water
    without moving.
"Drown-proofing," they called it.
Said it could hold you up for hours.
These are the days that slow
to the pace of glass,
the world outside a silent, lazy smudge
on the horizon somewhere.
"After my son was born," a friend told me,
"in those first few months, whenever he was asleep,
I'd spend hours putting on makeup,
just so I could touch my own face again,
just so I knew I was there."

In the dreams they are green and determined,
growing larger by the minute, and there's something
I need to warn them about before it's too late,
but they go on ripening without me.
So far, I always find myself awake
before anything else happens,
hands in the dry night, exploring the bed
for a mess of pulp and seeds.

Meanwhile, my son turns ten this summer.
Every morning, he plays baseball in the park next door,
leaving me quiet for coffee and the paper.
But it never works. It's his voice, rising
through the noise of the game, that shapes me still,
the way, years earlier, his turning knotted my belly,
the kick under my ribs, aimed at the heart.
When I take my coffee to the bleachers, he ignores me.
He's the smallest boy on his team, but he's got a good arm.

The coach gives him third base, usually, or shortstop.
Right field is a demotion. I can tell he feels it
by his walk, though his face shows nothing.
It's like the sadness in his wrists when he's up to bat,
knowing he'll manage a good base hit, probably, but never
    a home run.
He's the kind of player every coach needs on the team
and, watching him stretch for a fly ball, I can see
how I'm the one who needs to grow up.
I carried him like the future, unmarked, malleable,
but what I gave birth to isn't like that at all,
isn't a life I can decide for any more.
This is what my son knows already;
he just wants to get on with it.

What I get on with is this dream
where women swell up like melons,
ready to ripen or burst.
I want to believe I am dreaming for my friends,
for all the things I'd tell them if I could.
How they are bound by this birth forever
to the lives of other women, to a love
that roots itself as deeply
as our need for the earth.
I want to tell them this
is an old, old story,
but of course they can't listen.
They are ripening into their own versions of it
as if it had never happened to anyone else before.
These women I love so much.
Their recklessness. Like that fly ball
at the speed of light
stinging into my son's glove.

JEREMY AT TEN

This is the year you will be safest in.
According to statistics, that is,
those talismans I want to trust
like the newborn's caul that midwives saved
against a death by drowning.
This is the year you wear
like an Elven Cloak or Gauntlets of Ogre Power;
this is your Great Tree, your Wind Wailer,
the Bag of Devouring for your travels through the thick,
dangerous forest of my love.

And you are right to think it dangerous.
In our first photograph together,
you're still buried in me,
I am toasting you with a glass of wine,
a riotous madonna, almost as large
as I am in this one
where you hold my knees as I rise
into the sky like a tree,
("like a tree falling," you would tell me
later that year—I was teaching you how to skate
and slipped—"you looked like a tree falling.")
though you can't tell anything from these pictures.
Disguised as mother and son
we could be anybody's,
that's what photographs do,
they deliver us from ourselves
from the darkness their images depend upon.

But there were days when I couldn't stand it.
Your hands on my breasts,
my head filled with nothing
but tears and the smell of urine,
all those days falling in on themselves
one like another, to that afternoon
at the edge of the river, you were throwing stones,
the day I stood behind you thinking
I could push him in and no-one would ever know,
the need flowering as a dream flowers,
filling me with its desire,
a scent I couldn't separate from my own.
How that memory twists my heart,
bloodies my mouth, treacherous
and beautiful as Anat, the goddess
who destroys what she creates,
for this is also how I love you, Jeremy: so much
I could eat you alive.

This is why you must go
now, in the year you will always be
safest in, when the fish spring to your hook
and the earth turns up coins under your feet.
And it will begin in earnest then,
what the midwives mean
with their homely proverb
for every baby a tooth
the first gentle warning
that each birth is also a loss
we never touch the bottom of.

83

For where else can love be
but in this moment of letting you go, again and again,
the moment when lovers turn from each other at last
or the child turns to begin its journey into light,
the moment when we know ourselves to be unique,
mortal, separate, like everybody else,
the tips of our tongues, Jeremy,
each strand of hair,
our cells as constant as the stars
burning with their necessary song.

84

LEARNING FROM THE HANDS

They say it's in the opposition of the thumbs.
For all we know, whales sing in five-act plays,
but they can't write them down.
In a few million years—our wings slimming into arms
or paws flexing to fingers—we've made great strides
in the animal kingdom, most of it on our hands.

Some hands can see.
Those of the blind, of course, the delicate whorls
of their fingertips shining like eyes,
and maybe those of certain healers,
though perhaps it's more like sonar guides them
to the cells' cry for help; the hands of potters, definitely,
and wood-carvers, old men who can free
fantastic animals from glum wood;
but mostly hands, being hands, insist
that touch is the first mystery, wiser than sight.
Everywhere pregnant women place a hand to the belly,
listening for the first flutter-kick, the child inside
rocked by the warm walls of its mother's body,
stronger, even, than the sound of her heart.

85

All our lives, the hands of strangers feed us
and closest to our skin we wear
whatever their hands have learned, the small humiliations
they carry in to work with them each day.
We deliver ourselves to the hands of doctors
and carpenters, engineers, pilots, dentists, cab-drivers,
some guy tightening bolts on an assembly-line somewhere
stoned or hungover, angry at his foreman,
in love with the new girl in payroll
or just plain bored, we trust him
with our lives every time we start the car.
No wonder jugglers and magicians say
that magic is in the hands,
which are never really quicker than the eye,
only more sure of themselves.

This is how we live,
in a world run by thugs
who think a hand is just a weapon,
like the body, a machine for following orders,
filling the fields and oceans of the earth
with the ones that have refused.
This is what hands have become
after so many centuries, having to learn
how much they can endure
before the nerve-ends underneath the fingernails
stop screaming at the brain.
And something else the hands know
only too well: how often they must measure
the little they can do
against how long it takes.

We each carry our life in our hands—
the palm's cartography unfolded
for the fortune-teller, as if the future mattered—
our deaths, which belong to us from the beginning,
visible, necessary as the past
which nothing can take from us, ever.

There are nineteen small bones in the hand
and nineteen small muscles. *Eight muscles*
are inserted into the bones of the thumb.
All are used in combination
and all movements of the thumb are complex.
They can gouge a mountain,
put an eye back in its socket;
they are the needles thought needs to piece
the world together, the brain's light
threaded through the thumb;
or the heart's—hands are the only arrows
of desire that can reach what they want,
they mean what they can do
and no more, taking so many million years
to bring us here, our hands
what we have instead of wings,
the closest we can come to flight.

87